Mystery at Mt. Shiveer

By Ellis Byrd

Penguin Young Readers Licenses
An Imprint of Penguin Random House

PENGUIN YOUNG READERS LICENSES
An Imprint of Penguin Random House LLC

Cover illustrated by Karianne Koski Hutchinson

ISBN 9780451534491 10 9 8 7 6 5 4 3 2 1

"Welcome to day one of Jamaa's first-ever Winter Games!"

Cheers erupted from the hundreds of animals surrounding the enormous bonfire at the base of Mt. Shiveer. Liza beamed, lowering the conch shell Graham had modified for her to use as a megaphone. Her heart glowed with warmth at the sight of so many species gathered together, their enthusiasm obvious.

Bunnies and elephants handed out pom-poms they had made out of long, silky blades of grass painted in bright colors. Falcons and eagles swooped and dipped over everyone's heads with confetti clutched in their talons to sprinkle over the festivities. Kangaroos and koalas blew whistles, while lemurs and lions waved noisemakers filled with rattling pebbles. A group of penguins hopped on one another's shoulders to form a shaky pyramid for a few seconds before tumbling to the ground amid gales of laughter.

Liza raised a paw, and the crowd quieted. "I'm so excited for this event," she continued, her violet eyes twinkling. "And I know you all are, too. After all, we have much to celebrate! For years, we've worked together to clean Jamaa and repair the damage the Phantoms once caused."

At the mention of Phantoms, the animals grew somber. Liza surveyed them, her chin high. "Many of you here today were at our side at Mt. Mira when we drove the Phantoms away and prevented a terrible volcanic eruption. And some of you even fought with us in the first battle against the Phantom Queen, when we lost our beloved guardian spirits, Mira and Zios. It's because of their sacrifice, and your hard work and dedication, that Jamaa is once again a safe and beautiful place to live."

Liza paused, looking for her fellow Alphas. Cosmo and Graham stood near the front of the crowd, clutching noisemakers, along with Peck, who was easy to spot due to the pom-poms she'd tied to her long ears. Sir Gilbert watched Liza proudly from his place between the polar bears and snow leopards, while Greely and a handful of animals quietly sat on the edge of the frost-covered pine tree forest that grew at the base of the mighty mountain.

"Defeating the Phantoms hasn't been easy," Liza went on, and a few animals nodded in agreement. "Our success is worth celebrating—and that's what the Winter Games are all about! Over the next few days, you'll get to participate in all kinds of exciting athletic competitions, like speed skating, sledding, and skiing, and even a fun game of capture the snow castle. These games are a way for us to celebrate our incredible accomplishments, and I can't wait to get started!"

Cheers rose up again, along with the rattle of noisemakers and the waving of pom-poms. Liza noticed a snow leopard sigh as he batted a fresh sprinkling of confetti from his eyes, and she lifted her conch shell again.

"I'd like to thank the animals of Mt. Shiveer for their hospitality and patience," she said, smiling at the snow leopard. "The Winter Games have taken several months of preparation, and I know everyone here is so grateful to them for graciously hosting this event."

An arctic fox's head popped up in the middle of the crowd, his black eyes sparkling. "And let's not forget the Alphas!" he called with a mischievous grin. "After all, they're the ones who organized this whole shindig. Three cheers for the Alphas!"

"Hip hip hooray!" the animals cried. *"Hip hip hooray! Hip hip hooray!"*

"Thank you, Artie," Liza said, returning the fox's smile. "We can't wait to share all the activities we have planned with everyone."

"Oh, I bet there are lots more surprises in store!" Artie replied. Before Liza could respond, a giraffe near the back of the crowd gasped.

"The ice sculpture!" she exclaimed, straining her neck and peering at the entrance to the opening celebrations. Peck and Sir Gilbert had worked with a team of bunnies to carve an enormous statue of Mira, one of the guardian spirits of Jamaa, to welcome everyone to the Winter Games. Liza twisted to look, but she couldn't see over the rhinos.

"What's wrong?" Sir Gilbert asked, brows furrowed.

The giraffe's eyes widened. "It's . . . it's *melting*!"

"But it can't be!" Peck hopped up and down in an attempt to see the statue. "It's so cold out!"

"What if it's not the temperature?" a penguin fretted. "What if it's . . . Phantoms?"

Several animals let out cries of fear, and before Liza could say a single reassuring word, chaos ensued. There was a stampede as the frightened crowd fled into the woods, putting as much distance between themselves and the entrance as possible. Liza joined Sir Gilbert and Cosmo in trying to calm the animals, while Graham and Peck rushed toward the sculpture.

"We'll check it out!" Peck called to Liza, dodging around a charging rhino. "I'm sure it's just an accident!"

On the outskirts of the woods, Greely frowned as he murmured to himself. "Phantoms are unlikely, but I doubt this is an accident."

The arctic wolf at his side was silent for a moment. Snowflakes drifted down from the pine trees, blending perfectly with his thick white fur. "I'd be happy to look into it, if you like," he said gruffly. "I've learned much from you in the last few months, Greely."

"I appreciate that, Walter," Greely replied. "But I'd rather investigate this myself."

The arctic wolf smiled tightly. "We've been through this, Greely. You can call me

Walt," he replied. "And while I know you're quite capable, you don't know Mt. Shiveer quite as well as I do."

Greely turned to his protégé, considering this. The other Alphas had befriended many of the animals who called Mt. Shiveer home back when they'd first started planning the Winter Games. But Walt had avoided the Alphas, staying on the side and watching, instead of joining the crowd. He reminded Greely strongly of himself—someone who often worked best alone. But though Greely was still reluctant to admit it, he now understood that being part of a team *did* have some value. He was hoping he could help Walt come to that realization, too.

"A valid point," Greely conceded at last, his low voice barely audible over the retreating stampede. "Very well. Do a careful inspection of the entrance. Be sure to ask anyone nearby if they saw anything unusual. I will check on the other activities we have planned for today and make sure everything is still in order."

With that, Greely slipped between the trees and vanished. Walt gazed after him for a moment before making his way toward the entrance, his glittering yellow eyes the only thing visible against the snow.

"What a mess."

Paws on her hips, Peck surveyed the entrance to the opening celebrations. The beautiful ice sculpture of Mira that she and Sir Gilbert had been so excited about was now just a puddle of gray slush. Discarded noisemakers and whistles were scattered all over the wet ground, along with plenty of confetti. Next to Peck, Graham scratched his head.

"I could probably build something to clean this up quickly," he said, peering around through his goggles. "Some sort of super cooler to freeze this puddle, trapping the trash inside. Then we could just lift up the ice and dispose of it all in one go."

"That's a good idea," Peck told him. "But first, let's take a look around. Maybe we can find a clue that'll tell us how this happened—and who's responsible."

The two Alphas inspected the entrance. Peck checked under some bushes and sighed.

"Nothing here . . . Oh, hang on!"

A few feet away, something round and purple stuck out of a mound of snow. Peck hurried over to take a closer look.

"A handle," she murmured, brushing a bit of frost away. "Wait a minute, I know what this is . . ."

Peck grabbed the handle and pulled a giant, heavy pitcher from the snow. Then she spotted another one beneath it. "Graham!" she called. "Do you recognize these?"

A moment later, Graham joined her. "Yes, yes indeed," the monkey Alpha said, pushing his goggles up to the top of his head. "Pitchers from the Hot Cocoa Hut!"

"That's what I thought," Peck said, pulling out a second pitcher. "Two . . . three . . . there's gotta be at least a dozen here! And it almost looks like someone tried to bury them."

"Or maybe a few animals just brought some hot cocoa to the opening celebrations and forgot the pitchers when they fled." Tilting his head back, Graham squinted up at the tall pine trees. "Those branches are holding a lot of snow. Some could've fallen on them."

"True." Peck handed the first pitcher to Graham. "Still, they might be evidence. I think we should see what the other Alphas think."

When Peck turned around, she heard a light rustling sound in the bushes. A bit of movement caught her eye—a white tail, almost invisible against the snowy backdrop, whipping around a tree trunk.

Peck stepped forward. "Artie?" she called. "Is that you? You can come out—there aren't any Phantoms, it's perfectly safe!"

There was no response. Peck and Graham looked at each other, frowning.

"Everyone's a bit spooked," Peck said at last. "I hope Liza and the others were able to calm them down."

Graham nodded. "Let's get back to Alphas Hollow and find out."

Alphas Hollow was located inside an enormous tree with great twisting roots. A cheery fire crackled in the hearth, casting a flickering glow on the shelves and cabinets stocked with all types of tools, art supplies, and herbs. While Graham rummaged around one of the cabinets, Peck showed Sir Gilbert, Liza, and Cosmo the pitchers from the Hot Cocoa Hut.

Sir Gilbert inspected one of the pitchers. "And you believe the culprit attempted to conceal this evidence in the snow?" he asked.

Peck wrinkled her nose. "Maybe. Or maybe snow just fell on them, or got kicked over them. The celebration did get pretty rowdy."

"We don't even know if these pitchers are evidence of any foul play," Liza added. "What animal would want to melt that beautiful sculpture of Mira?"

Exhaling slowly, Sir Gilbert looked up at Liza. "Maybe it *was* Mira. Maybe this is another call for help. Another chance to rescue her, after my failed attempt last time. That blasted volcano . . ."

Peck put a sympathetic paw on Sir Gilbert's shoulders. Before the eruption at Mt. Mira, Sir Gilbert and Greely had made contact with Mira through a mystical pool, but they had been unable to help her. Sir Gilbert still took the loss personally.

Graham poked his head out from the cabinet, clutching a wood chisel. "It could've been the work of Phantoms!" he reminded Peck. "We didn't see any evidence that one had been lurking around, but we can't rule them out."

"But why would they melt an ice statue?" Liza said reasonably. "Especially with so many animals gathered nearby. They're usually more direct—surely they would've just attacked the crowd."

"Maybe there's another explanation," Cosmo mused. "Something about that spot . . . Is it possible the ground beneath the statue got hot enough to melt it?"

Graham scratched his head. "Possible, but unlikely. The ground was cool when Peck and I inspected the area. What would cause the ground to heat and cool so quickly?"

None of the Alphas had an answer to that. The silence was broken when the roots that formed the entrance to the Hollow began to shift, allowing Greely to step inside.

"There you are!" Liza exclaimed. "Thanks for checking on the other activities. Is everything running smoothly?"

"No problems as of yet," Greely replied, brushing the snow from his purple cloak. His eyes fell on the pitchers, and he approached the round table to join the other Alphas. "What are those?"

"Pitchers from the Hot Cocoa Hut," Peck explained. "I found them near the entrance."

Sir Gilbert cleared his throat. "We believe it's possible the culprit used these to carry hot water to the statue, then attempted to bury the evidence once the deed was done."

"Or perhaps someone just brought refreshments to the opening celebrations and dropped the pitchers when everybody started to panic," Liza added.

"Hmm." Greely's voice was dry. "Unfortunately, I believe Sir Gilbert's theory is more likely."

Liza's mouth fell open. "Why? These pitchers aren't proof of foul play."

"True," Greely conceded. "However, I've been informed that one animal may indeed have malicious intentions for the Winter Games."

Sir Gilbert's eyes flashed. "Who?"

Graham abandoned his hunt for tools and hurried over to the round table. He and the other Alphas stared at Greely expectantly.

The wolf Alpha sighed. "Artie, the arctic fox."

"Artie?" Cosmo exclaimed in surprise. "No way!"

"It can't be," Liza said firmly. "Artie's been a huge supporter of the Winter Games. You all saw how excited he was at the opening celebrations!"

"True, very true," Graham agreed, giving Peck a sideways glance. "However . . ."

All eyes turned to Peck. Her eyes were bright as she stared at the purple pitchers. After a few seconds, she whispered, "I saw him near the spot where the pitchers were buried. At least, I'm pretty sure it was him." Peck chewed her lip, looking around nervously at the others. "I called his name, but he was either hiding or he ran off. I—I figured he was just scared, like the other animals."

"And that could still be the case." Liza turned to Greely. "Who gave you this warning about Artie?"

"A reliable source."

"Yes, but who?"

"I am not at liberty to—"

"Greely," Sir Gilbert interrupted forcefully. "Now is not the time for secrecy. All of the animals attending the Winter Games could be in grave danger, and as the organizers for these events, their safety is our responsibility."

"So is the safety of my source," Greely replied. "Which is why I'm protecting his identity."

"Greely," Peck said quietly. "You trust us, right? Whoever it is, we'll protect them, too. But we have to be honest with one another if we're going to solve this mystery."

After a few long moments, Greely sighed.

"Very well," he said. "You all know my protégé, Walter. Mt. Shiveer is his home, just as it is Artie's. According to Walter, the fox has been acting suspiciously."

"Is he friends with Artie?" Liza asked.

"I wouldn't say *friends*," Greely replied. "Walter prefers to be on his own."

Sir Gilbert arched a brow. "Not unlike yourself."

The wolf Alpha's mouth tightened. "Actually, yes. He does remind me of myself. If he says we need to keep an eye on Artie, I believe him."

A pensive silence fell as the other Alphas considered this new information.

Before anyone could respond, a crackling noise sounded from beneath the table, followed by a high, panicky voice.

". . . breaking! Come quickly, please . . ."

"My walkie-talkie!" Graham exclaimed, ducking under the table. "I left one at each event location, just in case they needed to get in touch with us . . . Aha!" He emerged a moment later, setting a coconut shell on the table. A circle had been carved out, replaced with antennae, knobs, and a speaker. Graham fiddled with one of the knobs, then called: *"Alphas here! Can you repeat that?"*

A second later, the voice crackled again.

"It's the frozen pond—the ice is breaking! Please, we need help!"

"I'm on my way!" Peck was already hurrying toward the entrance, Greely

right on her heels. Her heart pumped wildly as she tore away from Alphas Hollow. She'd personally inspected the frozen pond for the ice-skating competition just yesterday, and it had been as solid as stone. If it was cracking now, there was no way it was an accident.

Her mind racing, she pictured Artie's fluffy white tail as he'd darted away between the trees. Could he be behind this, too?

Peck gritted her teeth and put on an extra burst of speed. She'd worry about Artie later. Right now, there were animals to save.

CHAPTER THREE

Dozens of animals huddled on the outskirts of the ice rink, eyes darting around nervously. A few snow leopards looked up when Peck appeared, followed by Greely, and they hurried over.

"It's the seals!" one told Peck loud enough for everyone to hear. "They're trying to cheat!"

Peck raised her paws, and the snow leopard fell silent. "Hold on—let's not accuse anyone without proof! What happened, exactly?"

The snow leopards led Peck and Greely to the edge of the rink. Peck was relieved to see the pond was still frozen. But after a moment, she saw them: zigzaggy lines forming a pattern across the ice.

"We were in the middle of the ice-dancing competition," the snow leopard told her. "It started when the penguins were performing their routine. When they finished, one of them noticed what looked like a crack in the ice. But we thought it was just a scratch from their skates."

Peck took a hesitant step onto the pond, and then another. She hopped up and down and shrugged. "Still feels sturdy to me!"

"That's what we said at first, too." The snow leopard pointed to another area of the pond. "Then the koalas danced, and then the raccoons . . . and every time, more cracks appeared."

"Hmm." Peck turned to Greely, lowering her voice. "Is it just me, or do those cracks look . . . deliberate? Almost like someone was trying to draw a picture?"

Greely frowned. "Perhaps . . . although it's difficult to tell from this angle."

"True." Peck glanced around, then pointed. "Can you climb up to that ledge? I want to try something."

She took another step out onto the pond, and Greely put a paw on her shoulder. "Wait. That may not be wise. It feels sturdy, but it *is* cracked."

"The ice is still thick," Peck replied, thumping her foot to demonstrate. "And I'm not heavy enough to break it, even if it's cracked. I'll be fine!"

She smiled at Greely, who nodded after a moment's hesitation. He headed up to the ledge, and Peck made her way slowly to the center of the pond. She felt the eyes of the other animals on her as she inspected every crack.

There *was* a pattern, but it wasn't the cracks themselves. Peck leaned closer to the ice, her ears grazing the frosted surface. The points where the cracks began and ended, she realized. *That* was the pattern.

Pulling out the paintbrush that held her Alpha Stone, Peck half slid, half walked to the first crack on the far-left side of the pond. She touched the paintbrush to the point where the crack began, then traced through the light layer of frost over to the tip of the next crack, straight down. Then a curve up to that point, another curve to that point . . .

She chewed her lip, carefully sliding across the ice, concentrating on the pattern she was beginning to see. Letters. Words.

A message.

Peck was so focused on connecting the dots, she didn't notice how much darker the ice was the closer she came to the center of the pond. Several animals were cautiously moving back onto the rink, their curious eyes following the bunny Alpha's progress.

"Greely!" Peck called, glancing up at the wolf Alpha as he watched her from the ledge. "Do you see what I'm seeing?"

Greely nodded, and Peck went back to tracing the last few letters. "*H . . . A . . .* ," she mumbled, skidding across a slippery patch of ice to the last dot. "*S*."

"Peck . . ."

Peck let out a shaky breath, hoping Greely wouldn't say the words out loud. If the other animals realized there was a message in the cracks, it might cause another panic. Especially *this* message.

BEWARE ALPHAS.

"Peck!"

Peck looked up at Greely, surprised at his sharp tone. She barely had time to register the look of fear on his face before a loud crack rang out, and Peck was suddenly airborne.

She flew high above the rink, too shocked even to scream. Below her, dark masses were emerging from beneath the frozen pond, cracking the ice and catapulting the smaller animals into the air, while the larger animals slipped and slid straight into the frigid water.

"It's the seals!" cried a snow leopard as Peck fell. A penguin screamed, "It's the Phantoms!"

And then Peck plunged into the icy water.

She thrashed and flailed wildly, her paws groping for anything to hold on to. Her thick fur protected her from the cold for a few seconds, but numbness quickly set in. Peck's eyes darted around frantically as she tried to figure out which way was up. One of the dark masses floated a few feet away, and Peck kicked over to it as fast as she could. She couldn't tell if it was a seal or a Phantom, but it was solid, and that was all that mattered. She reached out and grazed the mass with her paw. It was solid and rough, with a strange, porous texture. Peck felt a piece break off, and she snatched it as she drifted through the dark water.

A strong paw grasped her ears and pulled, and a second later, Peck broke the surface of the water. She gasped, shivering, as Greely set her down next to him on a chunk of ice floating on the pond.

Wasting no time, the wolf Alpha quickly leaped to help a struggling penguin escape the frigid waters. A few more of the large, mysterious masses emerged from the pond, breaking the ice into smaller pieces.

Peck looked around at the turmoil in astonishment: A few minutes ago, the peaceful ice rink was full of fun. Now, as Greely helped the final few snow leopards climb out of the pond, all she could see were cold animals shivering and huddled together. She dropped the porous mass onto the slab of ice and looked at it closely.

"Peck!" Greely knelt at her side, his eyes wide with alarm.

"I'm okay," Peck said, although she was shaking uncontrollably. Her fur was soaked, the water crystallizing around her nose. Greely swept her up and carried her off the ice rink, setting her down once they were near the edge of the pine forest. Before either of them could speak, a hushed but excited voice drifted through the trees.

"Ha! We sure showed them who's boss around here."

Another voice responded, this one lower but equally excited. "Sebastian, you were so right!"

Greely and Peck exchanged glances as the chatter grew more distant. The wolf

Alpha took a step toward the trees, then hesitated. Gathering all her strength, Peck got to her feet.

"Go," she whispered. "Follow them. Hurry, before they get away. But Greely?"

He paused, turning to look at her. Peck swallowed nervously, picturing the message in the ice. *Beware Alphas.*

"Be careful."

Greely met her gaze and nodded. Then he slipped into the woods, as silent as a shadow. Trembling, Peck began making her way to the rink. She examined the porous chunk of rock, a million questions flooding her mind. How had those rocks cracked the ice? Who had left that warning for the Alphas?

And perhaps most importantly: Who was Sebastian?

Greely crept through the forest, his breath visible in the chilly air. He could still hear the voices, but they were too far ahead for him to make out what they were saying. Quickening his pace, Greely mentally mapped out his path so far. The animals he was following had moved west, away from the ice rink, then altered their course northwest to avoid the hot springs, and now they were heading uphill . . .

. . . to the caves, Greely realized. Abruptly changing direction, the wolf Alpha darted between a cluster of juniper bushes and out onto the path before breaking into a sprint. The caves were a maze of secret passageways most animals avoided. Even those who lived near Mt. Shiveer feared getting lost in the dark, icy labyrinth. If Greely was quick, he might be able to cut them off before they reached the caves.

When he rounded a curve in the path, Greely's eyes narrowed, and he slowed down. A pair of arctic wolves were strolling toward him, deep in discussion. As Greely passed them, one gave him the side-eye.

"That's him," he murmured to his friend, who looked at Greely with an expression of deep suspicion. Greely continued down the path without looking back, his lip curling. *That's him?* What did they mean by that? Though he didn't care for it much, Greely had grown accustomed to the respectful attention that the Alphas normally received from other animals. He pictured the mistrustful way the arctic wolves had looked at him and his scowl deepened.

No time to think about that now, Greely told himself. His first priority was to find out who had sabotaged the ice rink—and more importantly—find out *why.*

Greely reached the caves and cast a glance around before entering. Shaking the snow off his fur, he hurried into the shadows. He would wait here, and as soon as they showed up, he would—

"So what's next, Sebastian?"

Greely froze, ears perked up.

Somehow, they had beaten him here. The mysterious Sebastian and his friend were in the caves already, their voices fading fast. Quickly, Greely moved toward the nearest passageway. But three steps in, he froze again.

There was a fork in the path. A fork that had most definitely not been here the last time Greely had visited the caves. Were there new secret passageways?

Listening intently, he crept down the tunnel to the left, following the fading voices. Greely could sense something else was off, too. The air felt physically heavier than usual in here, as if the forces of gravity were stronger, somehow. Greely didn't know what was going on, but he was going to get to the bottom of it.

Inside Alphas Hollow, Cosmo set a mug of steaming herbal tea in front of a still-shivering Peck.

"Elder flower and ginger," he told her kindly. "To help ward off a cold. We don't need you getting sick when the Winter Games have only just started."

"Thank you!" Peck smiled at him gratefully before taking a sip.

"Beware Alphas," Graham murmured, drumming his fingers on the table. "And you're sure there were no seals in the water?"

Peck shook her head vehemently. "No way," she replied. "There were these weird rocks. I can see why the snow leopards thought so—from the surface, the way they were moving looked like seals. Like they were swimming to the surface. Look, I grabbed a piece from one."

She showed them the porous chunk of rock. Cosmo's eyes brightened.

"Oh, that's a pumice stone!" he cried, picking it up. "It's formed from volcano explosions. This bumpy texture is because of bubbles trapped inside. That's what causes them to float!"

"Floating rocks?" Peck repeated, and Cosmo nodded.

"They must have bobbed to the surface and cracked the ice."

"But what are volcanic rocks doing in a pond at Mt. Shiveer?" Graham wondered.

Peck sighed heavily. "I think I know. Someone put them there on purpose."

"How can you be sure?" Cosmo asked.

"Because, well . . ." Peck pulled the blanket Graham had given her tighter around her shoulders. "When Greely pulled me out of the pond, we overheard voices in the forest. They sounded excited about the ice breaking—like they'd planned it. And one of them is named Sebastian." Peck looked from Graham to Cosmo, her expression hopeful. "Do either of you know anyone named Sebastian?"

Both Alphas shook their heads, and Peck's face fell.

"I just don't understand," she whispered. "Who in Jamaa would want to do something like this? I know Greely said we need to keep an eye on Artie, but I can't imagine he'd put so many animals in danger like that. We're lucky nobody was hurt!"

"Oh no, it wasn't luck," Graham reminded her. "You and Greely saved everyone. Something fishy is indeed going on here, but we'll figure out what's up."

"And we can talk to everyone who was there, too," Cosmo added. "Ask them about what you and Greely overheard. Surely someone knows who Sebastian is, right?"

"Of course!" Graham agreed. "Maybe we should visit the hot springs and chat with the animals taking a break in between activities."

"Great idea!" Peck shot to her feet, but Cosmo placed a paw on her shoulder.

"You need to rest," he said firmly. "Have another cup of tea."

"I can't rest now!" Peck told him, her eyes wide. "What if something else happens? What if—"

"Sir Gilbert and Liza are out supervising the games," Cosmo reminded her. "And Greely *will* find Sebastian—no one is a better tracker than him."

Graham patted the coconut walkie-talkie. "And if anything does come up, we'll be in touch."

After a moment, Peck sighed and sat back down. "Okay. But be careful," she added, and Cosmo smiled at her.

"Of course!"

Bidding Peck goodbye, Cosmo and Graham hurried to the hot springs. "Do you really think Artie might be behind all this?" Cosmo asked, glancing at his friend. "This is his home, his friends are all here at the games—it's hard to believe he'd put them at risk like that."

Graham frowned thoughtfully. "That's

the thing," he mused. "Maybe it's not Artie, *but it is someone*. Several someones, in fact—Greely and Peck overheard a few animals, including this mysterious Sebastian. The real question is *why*. Why would any animal want to—*egads*!"

Arms flailing, Graham slipped and fell, landing hard on his backside.

"Graham! Are you okay?" Cosmo exclaimed, helping the monkey Alpha to his feet. A gleam of something bright blue in the snow caught his eye, and he picked it up. "Ah, looks like you slipped on one of the pom-poms from the opening celebrations," he said. "Someone must have dropped it by accident."

"Not just that," Graham said, rubbing his head as he peered around the entrance to the hot springs. "Look, there's confetti everywhere. Food wrappers, noisemakers . . . Yuck, what a mess!"

Cosmo began picking up trash, his pointed hat slipping every time he bent over. Tigers, cheetahs, and an elephant chatted cheerfully in the bubbling water nearby, and other animals strolled around the hot springs and an ice-pop stand. "Do these animals not realize what they're doing when they litter?" he said in disbelief. "Pollution like this is how the Phantoms nearly destroyed Jamaa!"

"Well, it's not nearly as bad as when they poisoned the river water," Graham reminded him. "When all those crops in the Bunny Burrow were dying."

"True," Cosmo admitted, carrying an armload of noisemakers and pom-poms over to a trash can. "And it's definitely not as bad as when they blocked the reservoir in Kimbara Outback. Remember that vacuum you built to release the clean water?"

"Ah, yes." Graham smiled fondly. Then he frowned at the food wrappers crumpled at his feet. "Still, this is quite a lot of trash. Although I suppose it's to be expected with a major event like the Winter Games. Thousands of animals all crowded together in one place, you know?"

"That's true," Cosmo agreed. "But it's no excuse. Once we find this Sebastian and make sure everyone's safe, we should make an announcement about littering."

After they'd cleaned up the area, the two Alphas entered the hot springs. A lion and a polar bear sat at a nearby table, deep in discussion over hot-fudge sundaes, while a group of otters and foxes gathered eagerly in front of the ice-pop stand.

Graham and Cosmo stood at the edge of the water, surveying the animals. "Who should we talk to first?" Cosmo asked. But before Graham could respond, a sound caught their attention: *hissssssss.*

"Is that a snake?" Graham wondered, pushing his goggles up and squinting around. Cosmo didn't answer. Something was off; he could sense it. A smell like rotten eggs . . . the lightly trembling holly bushes . . . whispers from the leaves of the surrounding cypress trees, warning him . . .

"Look out!" Cosmo grabbed Graham by the shoulders and pulled him away just in time. A geyser erupted right where Graham had been standing, scalding water

shooting up into the sky. For a moment, silence fell as every animal turned to stare in disbelief.

Then a second geyser erupted in the center of the springs, and panic ensued.

The tigers and cheetahs scrambled to get out of the water. So did the elephant, nearly trampling his friends in the process. A third geyser erupted, sending the table and hot-fudge sundaes flying through the air. The polar bear pulled the tiger to safety, but backed into the ice-pop stand, knocking it to the ground. Yet another geyser erupted, this one blocking the exit, and now the stench of rotten eggs was overpowering.

Cosmo sprinted to the holly bushes and began whispering to them, circling the springs as quickly as he could. "We need your help getting this under control, my friends," he said over and over again. "Please absorb as much of this gas as you can without hurting yourselves."

Out of the corner of his eye, Cosmo noticed Graham frantically digging through the ice-pop stand wreckage. No, not just digging through it—rebuilding it, first the frame, then the motor, then the cooling fan with its giant blades.

After directing the panicked animals to take refuge under the cypress trees, Cosmo hurried over to the monkey Alpha.

"I don't think rebuilding the ice-pop stand is our top priority right now!" he called over the roar of the spewing geysers. Graham didn't respond; he was a blur of motion now, throwing ice pops over his shoulder as he put the parts together in a completely different way.

"I need holly leaves!" he cried, and Cosmo didn't waste a second. He ran back to the bushes and returned a minute later with an armful of the spiny, tough leaves. By now, the freezer was no longer a freezer, but a new contraption entirely, with the fan and thermostat surrounded by tubes and coils. Graham dragged the end of the longest tube over to the water and tossed it in, then grabbed the holly leaves from Cosmo. He shoved them in the contraption and slammed the lid. Then he cranked up the thermostat as high as it would go and flipped the power switch.

The fan whirred, the contraption shook, and the water bubbled around the tube. For a few seconds, nothing happened. And then, to Cosmo's amazement, the geysers began to weaken.

"How are you doing this?" he exclaimed, gaping as the geysers shrank to little squirts before disappearing entirely.

Graham wiped the sweat from his brow. "Quite simple, really. You had the right idea about the holly leaves. They're extra tough, capable of absorbing all of the dangerous fumes. They just needed a boost. Luckily, the ice-pop stand's freezer had all the parts necessary—evaporator, thermostat, defrost heater—all I had to do was reverse engineer them, then use the holly leaves as fuel, and bye-bye fumes!" He sniffed the air, and Cosmo did the same. "See? That nasty smell is gone!"

Cosmo breathed a sigh of relief. "Well, I don't know about simple, but that was *brilliant.*" He beamed at his friend as the other animals cautiously emerged from beneath the cypress trees. Graham flipped the contraption off, and everyone cheered.

Well, almost everyone. Cosmo couldn't help but notice that the polar bear didn't look especially relieved. She gazed around the hot springs, taking in the destroyed ice-pop stand and overturned tables and chairs with a forlorn expression.

"Not to worry!" Cosmo called, and she glanced over at him. "It's perfectly safe now."

The polar bear laughed bitterly. "It's also a mess," she said, gesturing at the wreckage with a heavy paw. "This is my home, you know."

The great white bear lumbered off somberly, closely followed by her tiger friend. Frowning, Cosmo turned to Graham.

"She's right," he said. "The sculpture, the ice rink, and now this . . . It's not just that animals are in danger. Whoever's doing this is hurting Mt. Shiveer."

Graham sighed. "Perhaps it *is* the Phantoms," he mused. "Pollution and destruction is what they do best."

"No one has spotted any Phantoms, though," Cosmo said. "And don't forget what Greely said about Artie . . ."

"But Mt. Shiveer is also Artie's home!" Graham exclaimed. "Why in the world would he want to harm it, any more than that polar bear?"

Cosmo chewed his lip. "I don't know," he replied. "But remember, the Phantoms weren't just good at pollution and destruction. They were also good at turning us animals against one another.

That's why Mira and Zios made us leaders to begin with, to help unite Jamaa. Maybe . . . maybe Artie is working *with* the Phantoms."

The two Alphas pondered this for a moment. Then Graham shook his head.

"I just can't imagine that *any* animal would be rotten enough to team up with the Phantoms."

Cosmo looked around the hot springs, where the remaining animals were already cleaning up the mess the geysers had created.

"I hope you're right," he said somberly.

Deep inside the caves, Greely stood as still as an ice sculpture. He'd been listening intently for several minutes now, hoping to pick up the trail once more . . . but it was no use. The mysterious Sebastian and his friend were long gone.

Frustrated, Greely began making his way back to the entrance. But after one step, a new sound reached his ears: the soft padding of paws on snow. Greely crouched,

ready to defend himself—or to go on the offensive, depending on who was approaching. Every muscle in his body tensed as a shadow appeared around the corner, followed by . . .

"Walter!"

Greely relaxed, stepping forward to greet his protégé. The arctic wolf looked startled for a moment. Then he shook his head and offered a tight smile.

"Greely. What are you doing here?"

"There was an incident at the ice rink," Greely said. "I tracked the guilty party here." He paused. "And what brings *you* here, Walter?"

Walt blinked. "Artie," he said quickly. "A few foxes told me he was here, and I was hoping to have a talk with him. What happened at the ice rink?"

Quickly, Greely filled Walt in on the ice cracking, followed by what he and Peck had overheard. Walt's brow furrowed.

"Sebastian," he murmured. "I don't know any animals in Mt. Shiveer who go by that name. However . . ." He paused, and Greely waited. "It pains me to tell you this," Walt said at last. "It was only a rumor, but this *Beware Alphas* message clinches it, in my opinion . . ."

"Yes?" Greely asked impatiently.

Walt hesitated. "I have heard several reports of Phantom sightings, Greely," he said gravely. "It appears they're back. A few animals claim to have spotted them not far from Mt. Shiveer this morning."

Several long seconds passed as Greely considered this. "There are a lot of animals here," he said slowly, picturing the way the frozen pond had cracked. "If the Phantoms are indeed back, everyone is in grave danger. I will discuss this with the other Alphas. Thank you, Walter."

"It's Walt, not Walter." Walt hesitated, then sighed. "Greely, what happened at the ice rink . . ."

"Yes?"

Walt looked Greely in the eyes. "Did you see Artie at the frozen pond?"

"No," Greely replied. He'd had a bird's-eye view of everyone at the rink from his spot on the ledge, and Artie had definitely not been on the ground. Unless . . .

"He was in the woods," Greely realized out loud. "That must have been him talking to Sebastian about causing the ice to break."

Walt hung his head. "I'm afraid you might be right."

On the grounds just north of Mt. Shiveer, two enormous snow castles sat on opposite ends of a field. One was a stately manor, its wide walls topped with battlements made of solid ice. The other was impossibly tall and graceful, with a twisty staircase leading up to its frosty towers and turrets.

Liza stood in the center of the field. "Capture the snow castle begins in five minutes!" she called through her conch-shell megaphone. "Team captains, you have another minute to discuss strategies before you take your places!"

The raccoon in front of the ice manor gave Liza a salute before gathering his team into a huddle. On the other side of the field, a kangaroo called, "Thanks, Liza!" and returned her attention to the animals crowded around her.

Liza jogged to the edge of the field to join Sir Gilbert and Peck. The bunny Alpha had met the others after she was feeling better. As Liza reached them, Cosmo and Graham emerged from the forest.

Cosmo glanced around to make sure the other animals weren't within earshot. "There was another incident," he told his fellow Alphas. "At the hot springs. Geysers erupting everywhere! Thanks to Graham's quick thinking, we managed to stop them before any animals were hurt."

"Did you see anyone suspicious in the area?" Liza asked immediately, but both Graham and Cosmo shook their heads.

Sir Gilbert frowned deeply. "And there's

been no word from Greely?"

"Nothing," Peck replied, pointing to the coconut walkie-talkie Graham had placed under a nearby pine tree. "Not yet, anyway. But if anyone can track whoever this Sebastian is, it's Greely."

Liza leaned on her walking stick and surveyed the field. "For now, let's just make sure this game stays safe. It's the only event going on right now because so many animals wanted to participate."

"I personally inspected both castles," Sir Gilbert added. "As well as the snowball launchers Graham built. Everything is in perfect condition."

Peck opened her mouth as if she wanted to say something, then pressed her lips together. Liza gave her a questioning look, and Peck sighed.

"It's just . . . ," she said hesitantly. "Well, I inspected the ice rink, too. But I didn't spot those pumice stones, and that put a lot of animals in danger."

An uncomfortable silence fell. Then Liza cleared her throat.

"Well, if anyone—or any*thing*—tries to disrupt this event," she told them confidently, "they'll find themselves contending with the five of us. Let's spread out around the field. Everyone keep your eyes peeled for anything unusual."

Once the Alphas had taken their places, Liza raised the conch-shell megaphone to her mouth again. "Captains, are you ready?" she called, and the raccoon and kangaroo both waved in response. "Capture the snow castle will begin on my mark. Three, two, one . . . *go*!"

With cheers and shouts, the two teams raced toward each other. Despite her worries, Liza couldn't help but smile as she watched the animals laughing, throwing snowballs, and chasing one another around the field. Every half a minute, the automatic launchers Graham had installed behind each castle's walls would fling snowballs out over the field, sending opposing team members running for cover.

"Defense! Defense!" the kangaroo cried as a bunny scurried up the castle's icy staircase. An eagle swooped out of one of its towers, chasing the bunny back down. As the game continued, Liza began to relax. A tiny piece of ice zipped past her face, and a second whizzed by her ear. Liza frowned, squinting up at the sky. Was it hailing? There weren't any clouds . . .

Just then, a cry of pain jolted Liza from her thoughts. A lemur was pointing to a snowball on the ground.

"That's solid ice!" he yelped, rubbing his head. "The other team is cheating!"

Before anyone could respond, another hail of snowballs flew over the ice manor's wall. Liza could tell they weren't lightly packed snow, but hard, heavy ice.

"Look out!" she called, brandishing her staff as she raced for the field. But within seconds, Liza was caught in a hailstorm of flying ice. She fell to the ground helplessly, covering her head with her arms.

Across the field, Peck gasped. "Liza!" she cried, racing toward her friend. Sir Gilbert hesitated, his eyes sweeping over the scene. "Graham, take the ice manor," he said. "Cosmo, the snow palace. Dismantle the launchers as quickly as you can. Go!"

They nodded before racing in opposite directions. Sir Gilbert charged after Peck, who had just reached the spot where Liza lay curled up on the ground. A rock-hard ball of ice slammed into the ground inches from where Sir Gilbert stood, but he barely noticed. Through the flurry of ice and snow, he spotted a message carved into the highest turret of the taller snow castle. A message that most certainly had not been there when the game had begun.

Beware Alphas.

Growling in frustration, Sir Gilbert hurried over to Liza and Peck. He swept his cloak over their heads, protecting them from the ice balls.

A moment later, Graham emerged from behind the ice manor and gave Sir Gilbert the thumbs-up. Over by the other castle, Cosmo hurried toward a dazed-looking sloth.

"All clear!" he called, helping the sloth to his feet. Sir Gilbert lowered his cloak, and Peck handed Liza her staff. Animals who had taken shelter in the snow castles or under the trees emerged, gazing around uncertainly and talking in hushed voices. The kangaroo captain looked over at the Alphas, her expression anxious.

"What happened, Liza?" she said, and the chatter ceased. "What's wrong with the snowball launchers?"

"I'm not sure," Liza replied honestly. "But rest assured, we'll find out."

The animals looked far from reassured. Liza turned to her fellow Alphas, trying not to betray how worried she felt.

"That's the fourth crisis so far," she whispered. "Whatever's happening, it's part of a plan. We have to do something. Otherwise the animals are going to be too scared to stay for the rest of the games."

"I can't say I'd blame them," Cosmo added. "Graham's contraptions have never malfunctioned like that before."

"They didn't malfunction." Sir Gilbert's voice was so low, it was barely audible, and the other Alphas leaned closer to hear. "They were tampered with. Look." He pointed to the highest turret of the taller snow castle.

Peck's eyes widened. "*Beware Alphas*—just like at the ice rink!"

Liza gripped her staff. "We need to find this Sebastian. And fast."

"There *is* no Sebastian."

Peck folded her arms, staring at her fellow Alphas. They were seated around the table in Alphas Hollow. This was their first meeting since the incident at the capture-the-snow-castle game two days ago. They'd been working overtime, overseeing the events and questioning every participant about Sebastian. Not a single animal knew anyone by that name.

Liza sighed, scanning her checklist for the dozenth time. "I admit, it's unusual that no one's heard of him, but he must *exist.*"

"What I mean is, there's no animal named Sebastian," Peck told her. "Not in Mt. Shiveer. Maybe not in all of Jamaa. There are so many different species here, and if none of them knows who he is . . ."

Cosmo cleared his throat. "Maybe he isn't an animal."

He and Graham exchanged a look. Peck shifted uneasily. "What do you mean?"

"Maybe . . ." Cosmo sighed. "Maybe he's a Phantom."

An uneasy silence fell. Sir Gilbert was the first to speak.

"I'll admit, I was skeptical that Phantoms were responsible for these incidents," he said. "Staying hidden in the shadows is highly out of character for them. But after seeing that message on the snow castle—"

"The same message from the ice rink," Peck cut in.

"Precisely," Sir Gilbert agreed. "Twice, we have been given a message. *Beware Alphas.* We must heed this message. Perhaps we have not laid eyes on Phantoms, but that does not mean Phantoms are not involved."

Graham, who had been fiddling with one of the coconut walkie-talkies, paused and looked up. "I agree, I really do," he told Sir Gilbert. "But the last two days have been perfectly peaceful. Not a single disruption. Cosmo scouted out the area around Mt. Shiveer, and there's no sign of Phantoms, despite what Walt heard. If

Phantoms are involved, why have they suddenly gone quiet?"

"But if Phantoms aren't involved," Liza countered, "the only other conclusion is that animals are sabotaging the games. What I can't figure out is *why*."

After a long silence, Greely spoke up for the first time since the meeting had begun.

"Phantoms could be involved, but that doesn't mean animals aren't working with them," he said. "Walter and I have kept close tabs on Artie since the ice-rink incident. He has participated in a few games, and I spotted him in the crowd at the snowboarding event yesterday. Then, last night, Walter followed Artie into the caves but lost him, and spent nearly three hours looking for him." Greely paused, exchanging a look with Sir Gilbert. "Perhaps the peace of the last two days is because the next disruption requires more planning. Meaning it could be even more dangerous than what we have witnessed so far."

Sir Gilbert nodded. "Agreed. We should spread out today and carefully monitor each event."

"There are walkie-talkies at every station," Liza added, standing. "Let's check in every hour." Pushing the checklist aside, she consulted the Winter Games schedule. "Sir Gilbert, why don't you accompany me to the snowman building activity? Greely and Peck, you can take the frozen football match. Cosmo and Graham, the ice slide opens in an hour—until then, can you patrol the grounds?"

"Roger that!" Cosmo said cheerfully, hopping off his mat. The Alphas left the

Hollow together, splitting off into pairs to head to their assigned zones.

"Want to go to the Hot Cocoa Hut first?" Cosmo asked Graham as they walked through the snowy woods. "I bet a few animals are hanging around there. We could talk to them and find out if anyone has seen anything suspicious this morning."

"Good idea," Graham agreed, brushing a few snowflakes off his shoulders. "And a mug of cocoa isn't a bad idea, either!"

The delicious scent of sweet, melting chocolate greeted them, warming Cosmo from his ears to his toes. He breathed in deeply and looked around. Several penguins were gathered around a table in the corner, chatting and laughing. After getting two cocoas, Graham and Cosmo headed over to join them.

"And then there was a loud crack!" One of the penguins had hopped up onto his chair while the others listened with rapt attention. "And the ice I was standing on went *sideways*!" He tilted his chair back, wobbling precariously, and several penguins gasped. "And for just a moment, I looked straight down into the frozen pond, and there in the water was—"

"Well, it wasn't frozen no more, was it?" a particularly short, squat penguin piped up. "If you looked into the water, I mean."

Righting his chair, the first penguin scowled and crossed his flippers. The tiny tuft of yellow feathers on top of his head fluttered as he turned to the squat penguin. "Look here, Nobu. Are *you* telling this story? Were *you* at the ice rink? Did *you* almost get seriously injured?"

Next to Nobu, a penguin with white-rimmed eyes grinned mischievously. "Injured by falling in freezing water, Shackleton?" she asked slyly. "Did you forget you were a penguin?"

Everyone snickered, and Shackleton's scowl deepened. "Very funny, Lois. But I wasn't talking about the water. I was talking about . . . the *seal*."

At that, a hush fell over the group. Pleased, Shackleton continued his story.

"The biggest seal I ever saw," he went on in hushed tones. "Bigger than two elephants, it was! Broke the ice, then lurked under the water, waiting for that poor bunny Alpha to fall in."

Nobu shivered. Lois frowned, but said nothing, and Shackleton went on.

"I slipped down the broken ice and

dove beneath the surface," he said, spreading his flippers for effect. "I saw Peck in the distance, sinking in the water. Got right up next to that seal, she did, before Greely pulled her to safety."

Murmurs and whispers broke out, and Cosmo and Graham shared a glance. The penguins were so captivated by Shackleton's story, no one had noticed them yet. Clearing his throat, Cosmo stepped forward and smiled.

"Hello! We couldn't help overhearing, and we wondered if we might ask you all a few questions."

Some of the penguins, including Nobu, gasped in surprise. Shackleton's eyes bulged at the sight of the two Alphas, and he lost his balance, toppling to the ground. The mood shifted as everyone burst into giggles.

"Sorry, sorry!" Graham exclaimed, hurrying around the table to help Shackleton to his feet. "Didn't mean to startle you."

Shackleton mumbled something under his breath, brushing the snow off his backside. Lois leaned forward, her eyes shining.

"Is it really true?" she asked. "Did a seal break the ice?"

Cosmo cupped his cocoa tighter. "There was something under the ice," he told the penguins. "But it wasn't a seal. There were large pumice stones that floated up to the surface."

"What about all the icy snowballs during capture the snow castle?" Lois watched Cosmo carefully. "Do you think that's related?"

"I think it's possible," Cosmo said, picturing the warning carved into the snow castle. "Probable, even."

Lois tilted her head, her expression thoughtful. "And what about at the hot springs? Any idea what caused those geysers to start erupting?"

"Oh, you heard about that?" Cosmo asked, and the penguins giggled again.

"Rumors spread fast at Mt. Shiveer," Lois told him with a smile. "There's no keeping a secret around here. Not for long, anyway."

"Then maybe you can help us," Graham said. "You know this area, you know all the strange things that have been happening—so what do you think is causing them?"

The penguins all began talking at once, flippers flapping in their excitement.

"It's the temperature! Too warm!"

"Yes, that's it—the body heat from all the animals is throwing off the balance!"

"Disrupting the natural environment!" Shackleton thundered. "Have you seen all the *litter*?"

"I think it's the arctic foxes," Nobu said, his eyes darting around anxiously. "They make me nervous."

Lois rolled her eyes. "Everything makes you nervous."

"That's not true," said Nobu, then he screeched when a waitress put her flipper on his shoulder. Lois and the others burst out laughing, and Nobu scowled.

"Sorry!" the waitress exclaimed, taking a step back and holding up a pitcher. "Just wanted to see if anyone needed a refill." Several penguins waved their mugs in the air, and the waitress laughed. "Good thing the hot water is back, right?" she said, pouring cocoa into everyone's mugs.

Graham frowned. "Back? Was it missing?"

"A few days ago. It was the strangest thing," the waitress told him, wiping the pitcher clean with her apron. "I had a pot of water boiling, ready to make a big batch of cocoa. Went to watch the opening celebrations, came back, and most of the water was gone! About a dozen pitchers, too." Shrugging, she headed back to the kitchen.

"The arctic foxes," Nobu said again. "I'm telling you. I saw . . ." He hesitated, and Cosmo gave him an encouraging smile.

"What did you see?"

"I saw one," Nobu said at last. "Before the opening celebrations—an arctic fox with some of those pitchers. Told me he'd bought cocoa for his friends, but he doesn't have any friends, everyone knows that. I knew he was lying—and this proves it!"

Cosmo felt as if his heart had just dropped into his stomach. He glanced at Graham, who sighed.

"Do you know this fox's name?" he asked Nobu kindly, and the penguin nodded.

"Artie."

"We all know Artie," Shackleton said pompously. Apparently irritated that he'd lost the spotlight, he waited until every eye was on him to continue. "Crafty Artie, that's what we call him. But he loves Mt. Shiveer. This is his home. If you're suggesting he's sabotaging the Winter Games, Nobu, I don't—"

"I'm not suggesting anything!" Nobu squawked. "Just telling you what I saw!"

Shackleton rolled his eyes. "You saw someone bringing hot cocoa to the opening celebrations, that's what you saw." Turning back to Cosmo and Graham, Shackleton stuck out his chest. "If you ask me, no arctic fox is causing all this commotion. No animal, in fact." He paused, letting these words sink in. "The Alphas are looking for someone named Sebastian, isn't that right?"

"Yes," Graham said, squinting at Shackleton. "Liza said she spoke to all the penguins yesterday, and no one knew anyone by that name."

"Indeed I don't," Shackleton said, nodding. "But I got curious after Liza left. So I started doing a little asking around myself. Sent a letter to my friend Phillip, an otter over in Crystal Sands. And he told me he had heard of someone named Sebastian, years and years ago." Shackleton paused dramatically, lifting his head. "A *Phantom*."

Nobu let out a little screech and hid under the table. The outburst of chatter quickly died down when Shackleton raised his voice.

"Back in the dark days when the Phantoms were taking over Jamaa, Sebastian wreaked havoc in Crystal Sands!" he told them. "Specialized in manipulating and polluting water, according to Phillip. Sound familiar? The frozen pond, the melting sculpture, the geysers . . ."

His words were drowned out by the penguins, who were really riled up now.

"He's right! It must be the Phantoms!"

"That explains everything!"

"I knew it all along! Told you all yesterday, didn't I?"

Cosmo turned to Graham, his eyes wide. But before either of them could speak, a snow leopard burst through the entrance to the Hot Cocoa Hut.

"The ice slide!" he cried. "Something's wrong with the ice—please, hurry! We need help!"

The snow leopard turned and sprinted back the way he came, and the two Alphas didn't waste a second in hurrying after him. Cosmo's mind was racing as fast as his legs. Could the mysterious Sebastian really be a Phantom? If so, how was it no one had seen him yet? Phantoms weren't exactly inconspicuous in Jamaa . . .

Cosmo heard the shouts and calls for

help before they even reached the ice slide that ran down the side of the mountain. When he and Graham emerged from the forest, the problem was obvious: The slide, which had been perfectly smooth just that morning, had somehow sprouted giant, sharp icicles. Several bobsled teams were speeding down the slide, swerving and crashing into one another to avoid the unexpected obstacles. The base of the mountain was a long, long way down from where Cosmo stood.

"We need something to cut off the icicles!" Cosmo cried, turning to Graham—but the monkey Alpha was already sprinting toward the ski and skate rental booth at the edge of the forest. By the time Cosmo reached him, Graham had an armload of skates.

"The blades are sharp, sharp enough to cut the ice," the monkey Alpha said quickly, more to himself than to Cosmo. His eyes roamed around the area, taking in the slide, the bobsleds, and the ski lift passing high overhead. "But we don't have time to cut each one individually, we need a way to do this in one fell swoop . . . *swoop*!"

Cosmo blinked in surprise as his friend took off again, this time for the ski lift. Dumping the skates on a pile of snow, Graham swung himself up the lift and began climbing to the top. "Pull the blades off those skates!" he called down to Cosmo, who set to work immediately.

Seconds later, Sir Gilbert and Liza joined him. "Greely and Peck are at the bottom of the slide trying to slow the bobsleds with their Alpha Stones," Liza said breathlessly, grabbing a skate and removing the blade. "What's Graham's plan here?"

"No idea," Cosmo told her. "But whatever it is, let's hope it works!"

"Heads up!"

The three Alphas looked up just as Graham pulled one of the cables free from its pole. Gripping it tightly, he swung down to the ground and spread the cable lengthwise so that it covered the top of the slide.

"Two sleds!" Graham called to Cosmo as he began threading the blades onto the cable like needles on a piece of thread. Cosmo's eyes lit up, and he turned to Sir Gilbert and Liza.

"I know what he's doing! Can you two help slow those bobsleds down even more?"

Sir Gilbert and Liza nodded, their

Alpha Stones glowing as they hurried down the slope. Graham pushed a sled over to Cosmo on the right side of the slide, then sat on his own sled on the left side. They each held one end of the cable low to the ground so that the blades were spread flat across the slide.

"Ready?" Graham called, and before Cosmo could so much as nod, they were off.

The two Alphas zoomed down Mt. Shiveer on either side of the slide, gripping their makeshift cable blade. As the first icicle rapidly approached, Graham yelled, *"Hold on!"* Cosmo tensed, holding his breath—and then the blades swiped clean through the icicle, sending it falling harmlessly next to the slide.

"Wahoo!" Cosmo cheered, beaming at Graham. They zipped passed a slow-

moving bobsled filled with sloths, the cable blade slipping harmlessly under the sleigh. "It's working! Here comes another one . . ."

Whoosh! They flew past yet another icicle, slicing it down, and then another. The bobsleds had slowed to a crawl thanks to the other Alphas, and the teams cheered as Cosmo and Graham flew past. At last, they reached the base of the mountain and instantly began to slow down, their sleds eventually skidding to a halt right in front of the spectators. The animals whooped and hollered, waving pom-poms and shaking noisemakers.

Beaming, Cosmo hopped off his sled and turned to look back at the slide. Half a dozen giant icicles lay on the snowy mountainside, and the last few bobsleds were crawling toward the finish line. The other Alphas were hurrying down to join them, and Cosmo took a step forward. Then a flash of movement caught his eye, and he whirled around in time to see a pair of black eyes staring right at him from the bushes. A split second later, the eyes vanished, and Cosmo glimpsed a white tail whipping around a pine tree.

"That was brilliant!" Peck appeared at Cosmo's side, giving him a quick hug. "But I wonder how those icicles . . . Hey, what's wrong?"

Cosmo sighed, turning to face her.

"I just saw Artie running away," he told Peck. "I hate to admit it, but I think Greely was right all along. Whatever's going on . . . Artie's in on it."

Deep inside the caves of Mt. Shiveer, Artie hurried up a steep, narrow tunnel. He was panting, each short breath a visible fog in the frigid air. The tunnel dead-ended into solid granite—or at least, it looked that way. Casting a furtive glance over his shoulder, Artie tapped the secret knock as quietly as possible.

Tap-tap-tap. Tap. Tap-tap.

A moment later, the scraping sound of

rock on rock filled the tunnel as the newly installed hidden door in the wall slowly opened. As soon as the space was wide enough, Artie slipped inside.

The cavern was surprisingly large and dim, the only light emanating from the swirling purplish-blue portal on the ceiling. Artie's stomach clenched with nerves as he peered around, looking for Sebastian. There, in the corner—a single large eye staring right at him.

"Hello, Artie." The Phantom moved closer, two thick tentacles on each side grazing the ground. "How did things go at the ice slide?"

"Pushing those icicles up through that new secret passage worked," Artie said. "The Alphas were fast, though. Graham and Cosmo cut them off pretty quickly."

Sebastian's pupil grew larger. "If I didn't know any better, I'd say you sound relieved."

"Well . . ." Artie hesitated, then blurted out, "I *am* relieved. Those icicles were bigger than I thought they'd be—like giant spikes! Some of those animals really could've been hurt!"

Sebastian's tone softened. "But they weren't," he told Artie. "I understand your hesitations, Artie. But remember why you came to me for help in the first place."

Artie shifted from paw to paw. "Yeah, I know . . ."

"And everything's going exactly according to plan," Sebastian went on. "Using water from the Hot Cocoa Hut to melt that sculpture of Mira worked perfectly, didn't it? And the seals were the ideal scapegoat for the pumice stones beneath the ice rink, weren't they? Not to mention altering the temperature at capture the snow castle and the hot springs—and was anyone hurt?"

"No," Artie admitted.

"But are they *scared*?"

Artie sighed. "Yes."

"Which is the point, right?" When Artie didn't respond, Sebastian continued, his voice louder now. "With fear comes doubt—and that's what we need. For the animals of Jamaa to doubt their fearless leaders. The Alphas." He said *Alphas* with a sneer, and Artie fidgeted again.

"I know, I know," he said anxiously. "This is what we wanted. But still . . ."

He trailed off when someone cleared their throat. Turning, Artie squinted at the shadowy figure lurking just outside the entrance, and his heart dropped.

"Our plan is almost complete, Artie," said the new, gruff voice. "The closing celebrations are tomorrow—it's too late to back out now. Besides," the figure added, a hint of menace lacing his words, "with all these accidents going on, it would be a shame if one happened to you as well."

Artie's throat closed tight with fear, and his eyes widened. "What? But . . . but I thought we were friends!"

Sebastian chuckled darkly, but the figure in the entrance didn't. His yellow eyes pierced Artie, who suddenly felt small and unimportant.

"Why would I need a friend like you?"

With that, the figure slipped back down the passage, leaving a shivering Artie alone with the Phantom.

The rest of the events at the Winter Games passed without incident, and on the last day, hundreds of animals packed the clearing near the entrance to the caves, chattering excitedly as they waited for the closing celebrations to begin. Greely surveyed the crowd from the top of a rock, looking for any signs of a disruption—or for Artie. No one had seen or heard from the arctic fox since yesterday's ice slide event. And while nothing remotely unusual had happened since, something wasn't quite right. Greely could sense it. His eyes narrowed, his hackles raised and his every muscle tense and ready to act if necessary.

The breeze carried a familiar scent to Greely's nose, and he didn't budge from his position. "Hello, Walter."

His protégé chuckled, joining him on the rock. "One day, you'll call me Walt like everyone else," he said. "I've been patrolling the ski trails all morning as you requested, and I found something you really need to see."

Greely frowned. "Now? I need to monitor the closing celebrations."

"What about them?" Walt asked, gesturing at the front of the crowd where Sir Gilbert, Peck, Cosmo, and Graham stood watching Liza take the stage. "I'm sure five Alphas are more than enough to keep things running smoothly, right?" Walt paused, turning to face Greely. "I promise, Greely. You need to see this. Trust me."

Greely cast a last glance at his fellow Alphas, then sighed. "Very well. Lead the way, Walter."

"I'd like to thank you all again for making the first annual Winter Games such a success!"

Liza smiled out at the cheering animals, but her eyes sought out the other Alphas in the crowd. She couldn't help but worry that something would disrupt the closing celebrations—something much worse than a melting statue.

"Of course, we've had a few hiccups along the way," she continued, and murmurs rippled through the audience. "But we've also had a lot of fun! I think anyone who attended the frozen football match will agree that it was a real nail-biter, right up until that spectacular play by the koalas in the last few seconds. The cheetahs really wowed me with their performance in the speed-skating competition. And I have to say, I had no idea the sloths could build such incredible snowmen!" A few cheers and whistles sounded, and the sloths smiled languidly. "We've learned so much about one another, and I know I have a newfound appreciation for each and every species here," Liza concluded. "And now . . . let the entertainment begin!"

As Liza stepped aside, the penguins who had performed in the opening celebrations once again took the stage to much applause, launching straight into an impressive gymnastics routine. Even their pyramid, which had been shaky and unstable at the start of the Winter Games, was solid, and when the last penguin reached the top and executed a perfect backflip, the cheers were deafening.

"So far, so good!" Cosmo told Peck, who grinned.

"Yup!" she agreed. "Nothing's melting or breaking or erupting out of the ground . . . Compared to most of the events over the last few days, I'd call this a success."

But she couldn't help noticing that not all the faces in the crowd were happy and relaxed. There were tight smiles and nervous glances, and Peck knew why. After everything that had happened, it was hard not to expect one last disaster.

No sooner had the thought crossed Peck's mind than Artie stepped out of the woods, hurrying toward her.

"I don't believe this." Peck clenched her fists at her side, and Cosmo turned around to see what she was staring at.

"Artie?!"

At the sound of the arctic fox's name, the other Alphas turned as well. A low rumble emitted from Sir Gilbert's throat, and Artie flinched, holding his paws up as if in surrender.

"Wait, wait—please hear me out!"

On stage, the penguins launched into a dance routine, accompanied by a trio of kangaroos playing bamboo flutes. The noise of the crowd grew even louder, and Liza beckoned Artie to follow her closer to the edge of the woods. He seemed to shrink as the five Alphas surrounded him, his face contorted with guilt.

"After everything you've done over the last week," Sir Gilbert said, his voice dangerously low, "you have the nerve to confront us now?"

"No, listen," Artie pleaded. "It's not what you think . . ."

"Cosmo saw you fleeing after what happened at the ice slide." Liza looked at him calmly. "Have you been working with a Phantom named Sebastian to sabotage the Winter Games?"

Artie's gaze dropped. "I . . . I have. But—"

"How could you?" Peck cried. "You put so many animals in danger, Artie.

Including your friends."

"And why would you ever work with a Phantom?" Cosmo exclaimed in disbelief. "You know their only goal is to destroy Jamaa!"

"Mt. Shiveer is your home!" Graham added, gesturing up at the mountain. "Why would you want to harm it?"

"That's just it!" Artie said, looking from one Alpha to another. "That's why we did it! Look, the Winter Games were a great idea, but in case you didn't notice, *you* were the ones polluting Mt. Shiveer. The Phantoms didn't do it."

At that, Cosmo and Graham shared a look. Peck frowned. "Us? What do you mean?"

"What do I mean?" Now Artie sounded angry. "Look around! There's trash everywhere, confetti and pom-poms and empty hot cocoa cups all over the ground.

And after this is all over, you and most of the animals here go back to your nice clean homes. But some of us *live* here."

Liza looked pained. "I know this was an inconvenience for the animals of Mt. Shiveer, but—"

"It's more than an inconvenience," Artie interrupted. "You're harming our habitat! Just like the Phantoms. So we turned to Sebastian for help teaching you a lesson. He's good with water, he knew exactly what to do to ruin the events . . ." He bit his lip, looking down at the ground. "But it got out of hand. We never wanted anyone to get hurt. At least, I didn't."

Sir Gilbert narrowed his eyes. "You keep saying *we*. You mean you and Sebastian didn't act alone? Who else is working with you?"

Artie's gaze dropped to the ground. "Someone I thought was my friend."

Greely heard the distant cheers of the crowd far below as he loped up the path, his eyes on Walt. His ears twitched and he listened hard, half expecting the cheers to turn to screams. Something didn't feel right. He should be down there with the other Alphas, ready to protect everyone in case Sebastian and Artie had anything planned.

"Walter, I don't have time for—"

Suddenly, the snow rustled and shifted beneath Greely's feet. A split second later, the wolf Alpha yelped as he was catapulted straight up into the air. Snarling, Greely slashed at the ropes tightening around him. But it was no use. He was trapped in a net, hanging helplessly between two trees directly over the path.

Greely twisted around until he spotted Walt, who'd stopped walking and was staring up at him. "Look out!" Greely called. "There may be more traps around. Take care where you step."

Slowly, Walt's lips curved up in a smile. Or was it a sneer?

"Oh, I will."

To Greely's surprise, Walt turned and continued up the path, leaving him alone in the trap.

"Walter? *Walter!*"

Greely could see the anger in Walt's eyes as he turned back and growled.

"Walt! I've told you a hundred times, Greely . . . my name is *Walt*!"

"Walt?!"

The Alphas stared at Artie in disbelief. The arctic fox looked even more nervous now, his ears flat against his head.

"Walt was the one who warned Greely about *you*," Sir Gilbert said. "Right after the opening celebrations. Why would he do that if you were working together?"

"Because I was just a scapegoat all along," Artie said miserably. "I think that

was part of his plan with Sebastian—use me to throw Greely and the rest of you Alphas off Walt's scent."

"Greely," Peck said suddenly, her heart hammering in her chest. "We have to tell him, he's right up—" She stopped abruptly, pointing to the rock where Greely had stood just minutes ago. "Wait . . . where'd he go?"

A booming laugh began, distant but loud enough to be heard over the hoots and hollers of the animals. As the Alphas craned their necks, searching for the source, another noise started—a deep, rumbling sound Peck could feel in her bones. She squinted at Mt. Shiveer, her gaze traveling up and up and up until . . .

"There!"

A hush fell over the closing

celebrations as everyone looked at the ledge near the top of the mountain. A massive mound of snow was building up over the crest, growing larger and larger right before their eyes. And next to it stood an arctic wolf, his white fur making him almost indistinguishable against the snow.

Peck swallowed hard. "It's Walt."

"You Alphas think you're so smart!" Walt's deep voice echoed off the rocks surrounding the now-silent festivities. "But you're not clever enough . . . not even my dear friend—and *mentor*—Greely. In fact, I'm not sure why he was even chosen as an Alpha to begin with."

"What do you mean?" Peck cried. "Why are you doing this?"

Walt sneered. "You've taken advantage of your position by forcing these Winter

Games on the animals of Mt. Shiveer! You don't care about us or what you've done to our land. But Sebastian does."

A few arctic animals in the crowd nodded in agreement, and Peck shivered. Next to her, Liza stepped forward.

"I understand you're upset!" she called, her voice strong and clear. "But whatever Sebastian has planned, it's not the answer. Let's talk about this together—I'm sure we can work it out!"

Another laugh began, but this wasn't Walt. This voice was unfamiliar, high and cold, causing several animals to whimper in fear. Peck's fur stood on end as a Phantom appeared at the top of the mound of snow, his eye blinking slowly as he gazed down at the ruined festivities. In one tentacle, he gripped a net—and inside the net, a large wolf struggled to get free.

"Greely!" Peck cried, fear seizing her heart. "Let him *go*!"

Sebastian raised his tentacles, and a powerful wind began to blow. Walt remained by the Phantom's side, though his expression was suddenly wary. Inside the net, Greely continued to struggle and snarl. A second later, the mound of snow shifted forward and began to spill off the ledge.

"Avalanche!" Sir Gilbert roared, and the scene turned to mayhem. The tiger Alpha raced forward with Liza right behind him. Peck sprinted up the path to the ledge as fast as her legs would carry her. She could still hear Greely's snarls over all the commotion.

"Can I help?" Artie called.

"You've done enough!" Peck cried, not bothering to look back. But she could hear the arctic fox racing after her, anyway.

Graham and Cosmo joined Sir Gilbert and Liza. They felt the power of their Alpha Stones flowing through them as they tried to slow the progress of the avalanche. But despite their best efforts, the avalanche was too big and too powerful. The enormous wave of snow was still making its way toward them, growing larger by the second.

"What can we do?" cried a lemur in despair.

A penguin glanced around, and his eyes lit up. "The stage!" he squawked, flapping his flippers to get everyone's attention. "We can use the stage as a wall!"

While the Alphas focused on stopping

the avalanche, the other animals rushed to the stage. Several rhinos hooked their horns underneath one end, and a group of elephants grabbed the other end with their trunks. They waited until the rest of the animals were in place, paws and wings all ready to lift the heavy stage. Then one of the rhinos called:

"One . . . two . . . three . . . *push*!"

Together, the animals heaved the stage onto its side. Eagles and falcons hovered in the air, steadying it with their talons so that it remained upright. A moment later, the massive wave of snow rolled past the Alphas, heading right for the makeshift wall.

"Hold steady!" Shackleton cried, pressing his back to the stage. The animals braced themselves, and the roar grew deafening as tons and tons of snow approached. The avalanche cast a shadow over them, and then—*thud.*

Silence.

For a few seconds, everyone remained frozen in place. Then an elephant peeked over the wall.

"It worked!" she cried. "Look!"

On the other side of the upright stage was a gigantic pile of snow. The animals backed away tentatively, but their wall didn't budge.

"We did it!" The penguins high-fived, laughing. "We really did it!"

A roar of anger sounded from the ledge. Everyone looked up to see Sebastian glaring down at them, clearly furious. Walt stood at Sebastian's side, but he was gazing down at the animals, his yellow eyes wide with astonishment. Greely was still trapped in the net, which Sebastian had pulled so tight, Greely could barely move. Peck and Artie were nowhere to be seen.

As the animals watched, a portal began to open right behind Sebastian. With a cruel smile, the Phantom grabbed Greely's net and began dragging him toward the dark, swirling cloud.

"He's taking Greely into the portal!" Cosmo cried, and the Alphas raced up the path as fast as they could.

"Sebastian! What are you doing?" Walt exclaimed, the confusion evident on his face. He took a step toward the portal. Behind the Phantom, Greely gnawed furiously at his net, working at a hole with his teeth.

"Don't you get it, Walt?" Sebastian sneered, gesturing down at the halted avalanche below. "The Alphas foiled our plans. They must be punished." His beady

eye narrowed as he looked down at Greely. "Losing one of their own is a good start, don't you think?"

"But we made our point," Walt said. "The Alphas disrespected our land, and we ruined their event. I—"

"*You* and your concerns about the Winter Games was never the point," Sebastian snapped, moving closer to Walt.

The wind whistled through the trees, the only sound on the otherwise silent ledge. Even Greely had stopped biting the net. He and Sebastian were both watching Walt, waiting to see what he'd do. Then a soft but determined voice behind Walt said:

"You're right, Walt. About how the Winter Games have been bad for Mt. Shiveer."

Walt's jaw tensed as Liza appeared

at his side. When he didn't respond, Liza continued.

"I understand your frustration, I really do," she said. "But, Walt, this has gone too far. Don't be swayed by Sebastian. He's a Phantom, and all they want is destruction and ruin."

Sir Gilbert emerged from a thicket of trees and crept closer to Sebastian, ready to pounce. Walt noticed Sebastian's eye dart nervously from the tiger Alpha to Cosmo and Graham, who were hurrying up the path and had nearly reached the ledge.

What Sebastian didn't see was Peck and Artie, slowly and stealthily making their way toward Greely.

"Is it true?" Walt asked Sebastian. "All you wanted was to destroy Mt. Shiveer?"

Sebastian blinked. "The *Alphas* wanted

to destroy Mt. Shiveer, remember?" he said. "I was trying to help you save your home from *them*, Walt." He held out a tentacle. "Come with me. I'm your friend—your only *real* friend."

From the corner of his eye, Walt saw Peck and Artie free Greely from the net. All six Alphas surrounded them now. They could capture both Sebastian and Walt easily, if they wanted to—and, Walt realized with a flush of shame, he would deserve it.

But the Alphas waited and watched. They were giving him a chance, Walt thought. He lifted his head and looked Sebastian right in the eye.

"Why would I need a friend like you?"

Shock crossed Sebastian's face, quickly replaced by fury. Quick as lightning, he flew into the portal. The dark cloud swirled and shrank to a point—and then it was gone.

For several long seconds, no one spoke. Then Greely turned and slowly began to walk away.

"Greely!" Walt called. The wolf Alpha stopped, but did not look back. "I . . . I'm sorry. Truly."

"We're sorry, too," Liza said, then turned to Artie. "To both of you." Artie's eyes widened, and he smiled gratefully. The other Alphas nodded silently.

Walt hung his head. "Greely . . . before I met Sebastian, I—I really did consider you a mentor. Can you ever forgive me?"

Slowly, Greely turned to face the arctic wolf. "You betrayed my trust," he said, his voice a low rumble. "I'm not sure you deserve forgiveness."

"He made a lot of bad decisions in the last few weeks," Peck said gently. "But just now, with Sebastian, he made the *right* decision. Isn't that a start?"

Walt gave the bunny Alpha a grateful look. Greely considered this, then turned to his protégé.

"I suppose it is," he admitted. "Very well. I'll give you another chance . . . Walt."

Walt blinked in surprise. "You . . . you finally called me Walt."

Greely's eyes glittered. "Well, there's a first time for everything."

Relief flooded Walt, and his shoulders sagged. More animals were emerging from the woods: snow leopards, polar bears, arctic foxes and wolves—the animals of Mt. Shiveer.

"We're so sorry for the damage our

Winter Games have done to your home," Liza told them. "But we'll clean up the mess we've made. If we work together, I'm sure we can restore Mt. Shiveer to what it was before all of this."

Walt looked around at the Alphas' determined expressions. And for the first time in weeks, he smiled a genuine smile.

"I know we can."

EPILOGUE

MONTHS LATER . . .

The spring sun shone down on Alphas Hollow, melting the last of the frost clinging to its leaves. Inside, the six Alphas sat at the round table over steaming mugs of cocoa.

"I saw Shackleton and Lois at the Hot Cocoa Hut," Cosmo told the others happily. "The penguins were all headed to the hot springs."

Liza blew on her cocoa before taking a

sip. "It'll be crowded! The grand reopening is today." She shook her head. "When I think about everything that happened during the Winter Games—those geysers, the icicles, the frozen pond—we're so lucky no one was hurt."

"Walt's road to redemption is a long one," Greely said quietly. "But his efforts to restore Mt. Shiveer over the last few months have been admirable."

"Artie, too," Peck agreed. "They both worked twice as hard as any of us at repairing all the damage they caused."

"Their actions may have been inexcusable, but they did have a good reason to be upset," Sir Gilbert mused. "All of the arctic animals did."

"And Sebastian saw that discontent and used it to his advantage," Cosmo added. "It was clever. It almost worked."

"I still can't believe a Phantom managed to convince an animal to work *with* him," Peck whispered. "They used to launch full-scale assaults, but now . . . they're getting smarter about their attacks. Sneakier."

Graham set his mug down. "Which means we need to be smarter, too," he said. "More diligent. More aware."

"You're right, Graham." Liza sighed, then smiled around at her fellow Alphas. "But no matter what's coming, I know we'll be ready."

CONTINUE YOUR ANIMAL JAM® ADVENTURE!

The story continues online! Uncover this book's code to unlock more fun on www.animaljam.com! Find the letters and numbers engraved on the stones at the beginning of each chapter and decipher them using the code below. Make sure to keep the letters and numbers in the right order of chapters one through ten!

Once you solve the code, go to www.animaljam.com/redeem or the Play Wild app to redeem your code!*

CODE

Replace	b	9	h	f	5	s
With	A	B	C	D	E	F
Replace	8	6	j	n	a	u
With	G	H	I	J	K	L
Replace	4	w	2	z	1	q
With	M	N	O	P	Q	R
Replace	v	p	0	m	i	k
With	S	T	U	V	W	X
Replace	u	2	c	e	d	t
With	Y	Z	1	2	3	4

**Each code valid for a one-time use.*